JAKE HOPE

CHEESED OFF!

ILLUSTRATED BY
GENEVIEVE ASPINALL

uclanpublishing

There are ~~mowses~~ mice in
this ~~howses~~ house

WARNING!

Do NOT say the word 'cheese'.
Cheese brings the ~~mowses~~ mice
from their ~~howses~~ house.
YOU HAVE BEEN WARNED!

'Time for party photos!
On the count of three,
everyone say . . .

Cheese!'

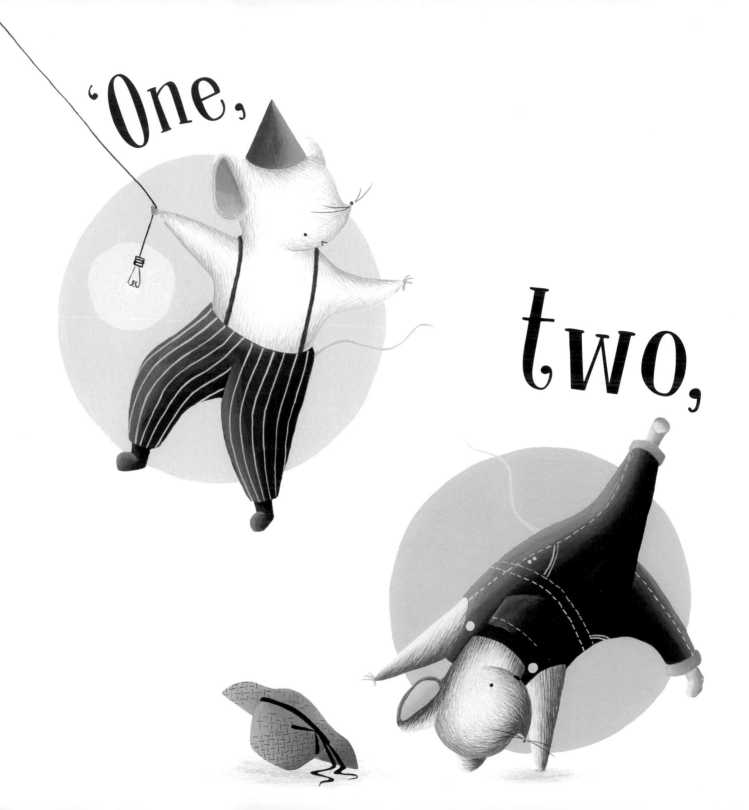

three...

‘Che

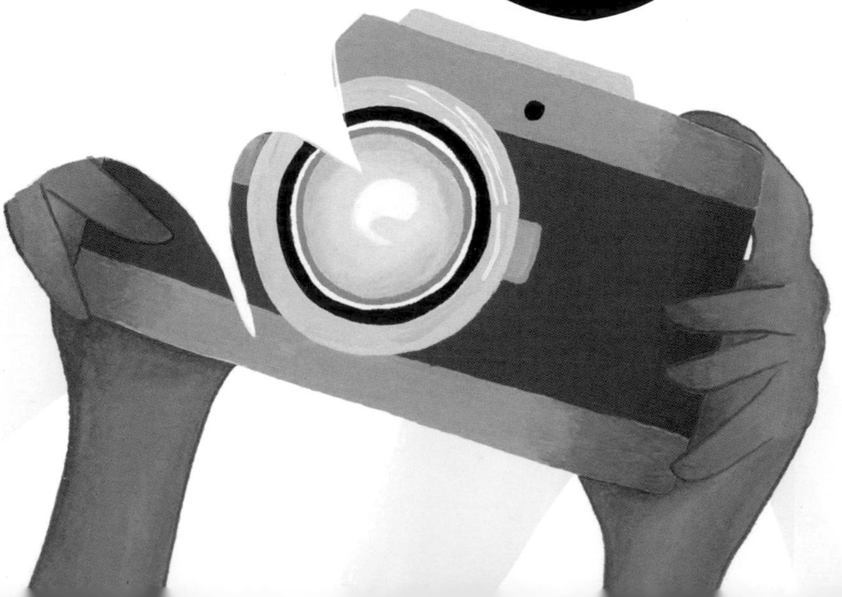

'Did I hear it?
I'm sure I heard it!'

Not a whiff,

not even a sniff . . .

. . . of cheese!'

'Happy Birthday!
You're the BIG Cheese now.'

'It's time, it's here!'

'Not so much as a sliver
or even a slice of
cheese!'

'No party is complete without cake.

It's everyone's favourite . . .'

'Cheesecake!'

'It is not the fault of the mouse,
but of the one who offers it cheese.'
Mexican Proverb

For Mum and Dad, with love and thanks. JH

For my family, for all their love and support, and
everyone who has encouraged me along the way. GA

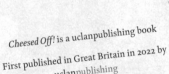

Cheesed Off! is a uclanpublishing book

First published in Great Britain in 2022 by
uclanpublishing
University of Central Lancashire
Preston, PR1 2HE, UK

First published in the UK 2022

Text copyright © Jake Hope 2022
Illustrated by Genevieve Aspinall
Design by Amy Cooper

978-1-912979-74-5

1 3 5 7 9 10 8 6 4 2

The right of Jake Hope and Genevieve Aspinall to be identified as
the author and illustrator of this work respectively has been asserted
in accordance with the Copyright, Designs and Patents Act 1988.

A CIP catalogue record for this book is
available from the British Library.

Printed and bound in Great Britain by Page Bros